The
Spotless Pig

First published in 2010
by Wayland

This paperback edition published in 2011 by Wayland
Published under a different series title in hardback

Wayland
338 Euston Road
London NW1 3BH

Wayland Australia
Level 17/207 Kent Street
Sydney, NSW 2000

Series Editor: Louise John
Editor: Katie Powell
Cover design: Paul Cherrill
Design: D.R.ink
Consultant: Shirley Bickler

A CIP catalogue record for this book is available from the British Library.

ISBN 9780750266079

Printed in China

Wayland is a division of Hachette Children's Books,
an Hachette UK Company

www.hachette.co.uk

The Spotless Pig

Written by Joe Hackett
Illustrated by Mike Spoor

WAYLAND

It was time for the cross-country run at Animal School. All the animals were on the start line waiting for Mrs Hooper, the teacher, to shout, "Go!"

Patty the pig stood to one side, looking worried.

"Come on, Patty!" Mrs Hooper called.

"I don't want to run," Patty grumbled.
"I'll get too dirty."

The sky grew dark and it
began to rain. Patty went and
sheltered under a tree. She watched
her friends warming up on the start
line, getting wetter and wetter.

"I'll run with you, Patty!" called Latif the lion. "It'll be fun!"

Patty shook her head. She wasn't like other pigs. She couldn't bear getting dirty or wet. Patty tried to keep as squeaky clean as she possibly could.

So, Patty's friends ran without her.
They raced across the playground...

they sped across the wet grass...

and they waded through the
muddy puddles.

The animals were soon filthy and wet, but none of them seemed to mind. Tessie the tortoise won, because she could run the fastest.

"Yippee!" she cried, as she crossed the finish line.

After they had cleaned themselves up, Patty's friends headed off to their after-school clubs.

"I wish there was a club I could join," said Patty, miserably. "But everything is just too messy!"

"Why don't you join the Cookery
Club? I'm baking a cake," barked
Toby the terrier through the kitchen
window. There was a big blob of
cake mixture on his nose.

"Oh, I don't think so. I might get
flour all over me," said Patty. "But I
will help you eat the cake afterwards."

"Why not come to Art Club with me?" suggested Oliver the owl. "We could do a painting together, or make something out of clay."

"But I might get paint on my hands, and clay is very messy. I think I'll just watch," sighed Patty.

So, Patty watched Oliver mix some paints to make green, brown and blue. He painted a picture of an owl soaring through the sky.

Oliver got some paint over his feathers
but it didn't matter. Mrs Hooper soon
helped him wash it off.

The next day, the sun was shining
and the weather was very hot.

Patty came to school covered in sun cream, carrying an umbrella to keep the sun off her skin.

"It's much too hot," she said, frowning. "I can't bear it!"

"I like the sunshine," laughed Latif the lion, as he chased a butterfly across the playground.

"Me, too!" cried Tessie, who was lying on the grass. "The hotter, the better."

Patty went straight to the classroom and stayed out of the sun all day.

But Patty couldn't escape the sun on the way home from school. Her house was on the other side of the park.

Patty sighed miserably and put up her umbrella before trotting quickly across the grass.

Just then, Patty spotted Toby the terrier going for a swim in the pond.

"Hello, Toby!" she called, waving as she walked over to greet him.

Toby climbed out of the pond and pranced towards Patty.

Then, with a grin on his face, he shook himself dry, spraying water everywhere!

25

Patty covered her face with her umbrella. "Stop it! I'm getting soaked!" she squealed.

Patty stepped backwards to avoid the spray of muddy water. She lost her footing on the slippery bank and down she tumbled into the muddiest part of the pond!

"I'm so sorry!" barked Toby, looking very worried. To his surprise, Patty didn't move.

"This mud is lovely and cool. For the first time all day I'm not too hot!" she grunted with pleasure.

Patty rolled over so that she was muddy from head to toe. Only her pink nose and ears peeped through.

"Getting dirty isn't so bad, after all!" she laughed.

"And now you won't need to wear sun cream," said Toby. "The mud will protect your skin."

The next day, Patty decided to join the Cookery Club.

"Who cares about getting messy?
Not me!" she squealed in delight,
as her friends clapped and cheered.

START READING is a series of highly enjoyable books for beginner readers. **The books have been carefully graded to match the Book Bands widely used in schools.** This enables readers to be sure they choose books that match their own reading ability.

Look out for the Band colour on the book in our Start Reading logo.

The Bands are:

Pink Band 1A & 1B

Red Band 2

Yellow Band 3

Blue Band 4

Green Band 5

Orange Band 6

Turquoise Band 7

Purple Band 8

Gold Band 9

START READING books can be read independently or shared with an adult. They promote the enjoyment of reading through satisfying stories supported by fun illustrations.

Joe Hackett was born on a farm. He remembers riding on a horse so big that he couldn't get his legs across its back. Now he lives on a little farm again, with his wife and dog Ozzie, who is small, black and brown, and loves best of all to go down badger and rabbit holes.

Mike Spoor loves being able to spend his days drawing the animals and pets of his childhood. He especially likes drawing animals with personalities that can be captured in his drawings, such as Latif the lion, Patty the pig, Finlay the frog and Tessie the tortoise.